D0718016

For Charlie Everton Bingham

Copyright © Hilda Offen 1992

The right of Hilda Offen to be identified as the author and
illustrator of this work has been asserted by her in accordance
with the Copyright, Designs and Patents Act, 1988.

All rights reserved

First published in 1992 by Hutchinson Children's Books
an imprint of the Random Century Group Ltd
20 Vauxhall Bridge Road, London SW1V 2SA

Random Century Australia (Pty) Ltd
20 Alfred Street, Milsons Point, Sydney, NSW 2061, Australia

Random Century New Zealand Ltd
PO Box 40-086, Glenfield, Auckland 10, New Zealand

Random Century South Africa (Pty) Ltd
PO Box 337, Bergvlei, 2012 South Africa

Designed by Paul Welti
Printed in Hong Kong
Typeset by The Creative Text Partnership in 24/28 Meridien Roman

British Library Cataloguing in Publication Data is available.
ISBN 0 09176423 8

A FOX
GOT MY SOCKS
Hilda Offen

HUTCHINSON

London Sydney Auckland Johannesburg

Yesterday
was washing day.

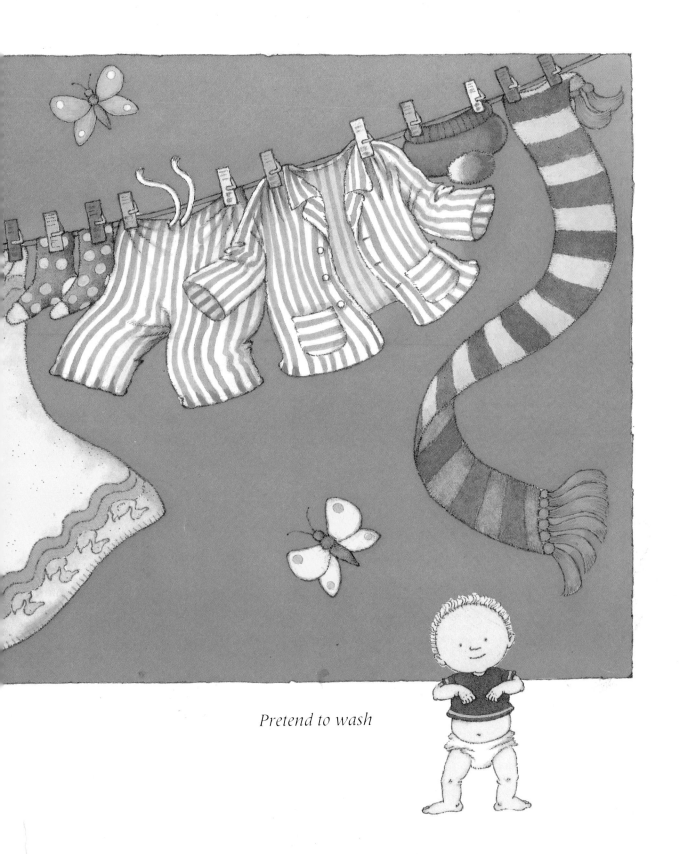

Pretend to wash

My clothes flip-flapped
and blew away.

Flap arms

A cat got my hat.

Touch head with both hands

A fox got my socks.

Touch both feet

A goat got my coat.

Pretend to do up buttons

An owl got my towel.

Pretend to flap towel

'Oh no!' said the pig.
'These pants are too big!'

Pretend to hold up pants

And the bear gave a snort:
'This jumper's too short!'

Pull jumper up

Two baby llamas
were in my pyjamas

Touch chest and knee

And where was my scarf?
Wrapped round a giraffe!

Pretend to wrap scarf

But the sun was so hot,

Fan face

I said, 'Keep what you've got.

Hold out arms

I'm perfectly happy ...

... to stay in my nappy!'

Dance around